The Speckledy Hen

The Little Grey Rabbit Library

The Speckledy Hen

Alison Uttley
pictures by Margaret Tempest

Collins

William Collins Sons & Co Ltd
London · Glasgow · Sydney · Auckland
Toronto · Johannesburg

First published 1945
© text The Alison Uttley Literary Property Trust 1986
© illustrations The Estate of Margaret Tempest 1986
© this arrangement William Collins Sons & Co Ltd 1986
Second impression 1987
Cover decoration by Fiona Owen
Decorated capital by Mary Cooper
Alison Uttley's original story has been abridged for this book.
Uttley, Alison
The speckledy hen. — Rev.ed —
(Little Grey Rabbit books)
I. Title   II. Tempest, Margaret
III. Series
823'.912 [J] PZ7

ISBN 0-00-194218-2

Made and printed in Great Britain by
William Collins Sons and Co Ltd, Glasgow

FOREWORD

Of course you must understand that Grey Rabbit's home had no electric light or gas, and even the candles were made from pith of rushes dipped in wax from the wild bees' nests, which Squirrel found. Water there was in plenty, but it did not come from a tap. It flowed from a spring outside, which rose up from the ground and went to a brook. Grey Rabbit cooked on a fire, but it was a wood fire, there was no coal in that part of the country. Tea did not come from India, but from a little herb known very well to country people, who once dried it and used it in their cottage homes. Bread was baked from wheat ears, ground fine, and Hare and Grey Rabbit gleaned in the cornfields to get the wheat.

The doormats were plaited rushes, like country-made mats, and cushions were stuffed with wool gathered from the hedges where sheep pushed through the thorns. As for the looking-glass, Grey Rabbit found the glass, dropped from a lady's handbag, and Mole made a frame for it. Usually the animals gazed at themselves in the still pools as so many country children have done. The country ways of Grey Rabbit were the country ways known to the author.

O ne morning in spring, when the primroses and cowslips were out in the fields, and the violets were blue under the hedges, the Speckledy Hen took a walk. She had decided to leave the farmyard with all its noisy company and live alone.

Robins, blackbirds, thrushes, fieldmice, and rabbits looked at her and shook their heads when she asked if there was room for her. So she left that field and tripped lightly across a narrow wood to a pasture, where a stream ran. In an oak tree was a round hole. The Speckledy Hen had seen it once, but somebody was living there.

The Speckledy Hen found the oak tree, and she walked round it, clucking softly. Nobody was there. She entered quietly.

Yes, it was a nice comfortable room, just the right size for a nursery.

She went to the field and picked a bunch of broom twigs. She twisted them into a little brush and carried it to the house. She swept out the dead leaves and brushed the walls. She tossed the little old bed out of the door, and threw away a musty blanket. Then she shooed out a fat spider, a family of earwigs and a beetle.

"Away with you," she cried. "I don't want any webs in my nice house."

When all was tidy the Speckledy Hen hunted for some nice dry moss, and she covered the floor with the carpet.

Satisfied with her morning's work, she went back to the farm and climbed the stair to the hen-house. She got together a bundle of her belongings, and stuffed a few things under her feathery wings. Then, looking extremely fat, she waddled across the farmyard and out of the gate.

"Where are you going, dear Speckledy?"
asked the Cock.

"That's a secret," said she, and the Cock
laughed and crowed, "Cock-a-doodle Doo."

He was used to the Speckledy Hen's
secrets. She always was a Hen who liked her
own way.

"Your bonnet's crooked," said he.

The Speckledy Hen couldn't straighten her
bonnet because her wings were hiding a
frying-pan, a sack of meal, a bag of Indy corn,
some little loaves and a teapot.

"I'll put it right my dear," said the Cock,
and gave it a tilt over her eye.

"There. That's better. You look very smart
for visiting, my love." He threw her a kiss,
but the Speckledy Hen said nothing. She
marched off into the field.

"Hallo!" said Hare. "Where are you off to, looking so handsome and fat, Speckledy Hen?"

"Off to make a secret," said she.

"Mind you don't meet the Fox," said Hare.

Further on she met Fuzzypeg, dawdling across the field, swinging his schoolbag.

"Good-day, Speckledy Hen," said Fuzzypeg. "Can I carry anything for you?"

"No, thank you, Fuzzypeg," puffed the Hen. "Have you been a good urchin, and done your lessons well?"

"Yes. I'm learning to read now," said the little Hedgehog proudly. "I can read long words like Treacle and Barley-sugar."

"There's barley-sugar in my pocket, if you can find it," said the Speckledy Hen.

Fuzzypeg stuck a little fist among her feathers and brought out a yellow stick.

The Speckledy Hen walked as fast as she could to the hollow oak tree. She panted through the little doorway and dropped all her parcels on the floor. She was so weary she had a little nap.

Then she busied herself, lifting the corn and meal and little loaves to the shelves, hanging her frying-pan on the wall, and putting her kettle and teapot ready on the stove in the corner.

She picked some primrose leaves and sewed them together for a pair of curtains, then she threw wide the door to let the sunshine in.

It fell like an arrow on a dark patch in the wall. It was a couple of cupboards she had missed. She opened the doors, and inside one was a store of honey, left by a family of bees which once lived in the hollow oak. In the other cupboard was a heap of nuts which a Squirrel had once hidden there and forgotten.

She peered at the back of the nut-cupboard and brought out a piece of leather made from a bat's wing. There were little hooks sewn down the side.

"It's a curtain to keep out the draughts," said the Speckledy Hen. She hung it over the doorway, and looped it back for the daytime.

Then, satisfied with her work, she went outside. A little stream ran close by and she filled the kettle. She collected firewood and gathered a few primroses. Then she made a comfortable bed for herself.

"How happy I shall be in my little house!" said she. She laid her first white egg in the nest and sat down to brood over it.

For ten days the Speckledy Hen sat there, and in the nest were ten beautiful eggs. She never went back to the farmyard, for her eggs would have been chilled. Everybody wondered where she was.

"Has anyone seen my Speckledy?" asked the Cock. "She went for a walk and never came back." He kept his eyes open, but although he went quite close to the little house, he never saw the small doorway with the bat's-wing curtain across it.

Little Grey Rabbit wanted to make a cake. She thought of all the spring flowers she would put in it, sweet violets, wood-sorrel, celandines. She wanted one of the Speckledy Hen's famous eggs.

Hedgehog called with the milk and Grey Rabbit ran to the door.

"An extra jugful, please, Hedgehog," said she. "I'm going to make a fine cake. Hare is going to the Speckledy Hen for an egg."

"Haven't you heard?" asked Old Hedgehog solemnly. "She's gone. And her frying-pan and teapot with her."

"Surely not," they all cried.

"Yes. Nobody hasn't seen her for more nor a week."

"I met her going for a walk," said Hare.

"Well, she never came back. And what's more, that there Fox has been about here."

"Oh, darling Speckledy Hen," cried Grey Rabbit in alarm, and Squirrel burst into tears. Hare went very pale.

"Don't take on, Miss Squirrel," said Old Hedgehog. "Here wipe your bonny eyes on my handkercher."

He dried her eyes on his big red-spotted handkerchief.

"I don't think the Fox has caught the Speckledy Hen, because she is far too clever for him," said Grey Rabbit.

"She's too cunning for that old Fox," said Hedgehog, nodding his head.

"Perhaps the Hen is hiding from the Fox and can't get home," said Grey Rabbit.

"I'll tell little Fuzzypeg to keep a look-out for her when he goes to school," said Hedgehog.

Now all this time the Speckledy Hen had been sitting on her eggs in her little warm house. She was happy and content. She chuckled as she thought of the day she would lead home a fine brood of chicks.

Through the wet grass walked the Fox, his nose to the earth. He sniffed and he sniffed, and he looked to right and to left, and he came to the little doorway. The curtain was drawn across and he lay down and waited till morning.

"Somebody lives here, and somebody will come out. Then I shall have company for breakfast," said he.

The Speckledy Hen was asleep on her eggs, but she heard the Cuckoo call "Cuckoo! Cuckoo!" and the Blackbird whistle it was time to get up. She drew back the curtains and peeped out. It was a beautiful clear morning.

The Fox walked round to the little doorway, and put his nose inside.

"Good morning, Missus," said he.

"Shoo! Go away, you bad Fox," cried the Hen.

"What bright eyes you have, Missus!" said the Fox.

"Shoo! Be off, you bold bad Fox!" shrieked the Hen.

"Won't you invite me inside?" asked the Fox. He knew very well he couldn't get his body through the little hole.

"Shoo! Off with you," cried the Hen.

"Goodbye, Missus! I must leave you as you won't be friends," said the Fox, and he hid behind the tree. The Hen put on her bonnet and crept to the door. She put out her head and a great mouth snapped at her. Her best bonnet was caught in the Fox's jaws.

"Oh, dear me!" she cried, as she sat down on her eggs again. "My sweet little bonnet! But it might have been my silly little head."

There was a pecking and a chipping among the eggs, then one by one the little chicks came out of their shells. She gathered them under her wings and sang softly to them.

Fuzzypeg was walking home from school, when he saw a little bonnet lying on a furze bush. Close to it was a long red animal, keeping guard. Fuzzypeg scurried away as fast as he could, with his prickles sticking out fiercely.

"There's a little bonnet hanging on a furze bush, father," said he, when he got home. "It looked like the Speckledy Hen's."

"Where was it?" asked Old Hedgehog.

"Near the stream in Green Pasture," said Fuzzypeg. "There was a fox hiding near."

"That Speckledy Hen has thrown her bonnet at him," said Old Hedgehog. "She's always been a daring female."

"I'll go and tell Grey Rabbit," said Fuzzypeg. "She will know what to do."

So off he ran to Grey Rabbit's house, and told them the news.

"I'll go and ask Wise Owl," said Hare.

"Take him a present," said Grey Rabbit.

"Your old musical box," said Squirrel.

So away went Hare into the wood. He tinkled the silver bell that hung from the tree where Wise Owl lived.

"What do you want? Have you brought a present?" asked Owl crossly.

Hare held up the musical box and waved his handkerchief.

"Please, Wise Owl! A Fox sits outside a house where Speckledy Hen lives and waits to gobble her up."

"A fox? I've no love for Tod Fox. I'll help you. Keep your musical box," said the Owl. "Somebody must read a nice story to the Fox. Something exciting so that he won't notice anything else."

The Owl dived into his library and returned with a stout little book which he tossed down to Hare.

"Read it!" said he, and banged his door.

Hare ran home, lollopy, lollopy, wondering who would read to the Fox.

Grey Rabbit and Squirrel turned the pages.

"Who will read it?" they asked, sadly.

"I can't make head nor tail of it," said Old Hedgehog, who had strolled in with Moldy Warp. "What about you Moldy Warp?"

The Mole shook his velvety head and sighed. "My voice isn't what it used to be, and my sight is dim. The Fox wouldn't listen to me."

"I can't read these long words," confessed Grey Rabbit.

"I don't know what these little black letters are," said Squirrel.

"It's a book about animals, I think," added Grey Rabbit.

"My Fuzzypeg can read," said Hedgehog proudly. "He's a scollard."

Little Fuzzypeg was called, and he said he could read the book. Off he went, and all the animals sat on the hillock to watch him.

When he got near the oak tree where the Fox was lying in wait, he called out, "Mister Fox. I go to school now."

"Oh, indeed," said the Fox haughtily.

The Speckledy Hen heard the voices and she peeped out. Around her sat the chicks.

"Mother, when can we go out?" asked the little chicks.

"Bide a wee bit," said she.

"I can read," said Fuzzypeg. "Shall I read you a tale, Mister Fox? It must be very dull for you waiting here."

"It is dull," agreed the Fox. "A good tale would cheer me."

"It's called 'The Fox and the Grapes,'" said Fuzzypeg, opening his book. The Fox kept one eye on the little door, and curled round to listen.

So Fuzzypeg began his story.

"A famished Fox saw some clusters of Rich Black Grapes," said Fuzzypeg.

"Rich Black Grapes," echoed the Fox, and he smacked his lips so loudly that the Speckledy Hen shivered.

"Rich Black Grapes, hanging from a trellised vine," said Fuzzypeg.

"Ah! They would hang there!" cried the Fox. "They don't grow on oak trees. They don't grow on blackberry bushes."

There was a minute's silence, and the Speckledy Hen hurried around, collecting her chicks in a bunch, whispering to them.

"You've never seen a vine," continued the Fox, turning his back on the little house. "I have. Down at the Castle, a trellised vine." He sighed. "Go on, Fuzzypeg. I like to hear a true story."

The Speckledy Hen cautiously looked out again. The Fox was curled up, listening to Fuzzypeg who trembled with excitement.

The Hen crept out, and all the little yellow chicks came after her. The Hen seized her bonnet from the furze bush, and started off towards home.

"Ah!" cried the Fox. "How I wish I had those Rich Black Grapes! How sweet they would be! But go on with your tale, Fuzzypeg."

Fuzzypeg went on, in a voice that shook a little as out of a corner of his eye he saw the Speckledy Hen slip behind the tree, and then walk off with her little tribe of chicks.

"He re-re-resorted to all the tricks to get at them, but he wearied himself in vain, for he could not reach them," said Fuzzypeg, struggling with the long words.

"Jemimay!" said the Fox. "It was just the same with me. I climbed on the greenhouse roof, and I couldn't get them. So near, and yet so far, as the saying is."

The Speckledy Hen was walking quickly over the field and all the chicks followed on tiptoe, their tiny wings outstretched and they never made a flutter of sound.

Fuzzypeg went on, as loudly as he could.

"At last he turned away, saying – saying – "

"Yes? What did he say? What did he say when he couldn't get the grapes?" asked the Fox.

The Speckledy Hen was now running at full speed with her chickens scurrying after her to the safety of the farmyard.

"What did he say?" asked the Fox again.

"He said, 'The grapes are sour, and not ripe as I thought,'" said Fuzzypeg.

"So it didn't matter very much?" asked the Fox.

"No. It didn't matter at all," said Fuzzypeg loudly.

The Fox sat thinking about this.

"How did the Fox know they were sour if he hadn't tasted?" said the Fox.

"I 'specks he said it to comfort himself," said Fuzzypeg, wisely.

"I 'specks so too. Thank you for the nice tale," said the Fox. "Who wrote it?"

"Mr Aesop," said Fuzzypeg.

"He was a knowing person," said the Fox. "He knew about us."

"I will give it to you," said Fuzzypeg.

"Thank you, kind Fuzzypeg," said the Fox. "I never had a present in my life."

Fuzzypeg tossed the little book to the Fox and walked away.

The Fox went back to the oak tree and sat close to the door. He called through the doorway.

"Are you all right, Speckledy Hen?"

There was no sound. Not a chirp or a rustle. He put his eye to a crack and peered inside. The room was empty.

Then he saw that the bonnet had gone from the bush near the door.

He galloped over to the farmyard, and there sat the Speckledy Hen with her family and the proud Cock standing near. Around her were Hare, Squirrel, little Grey Rabbit, Old Hedgehog and Fuzzypeg. They were all laughing and chattering.

The Fox watched them for a minute. He hungrily licked his lips, but the farm dog was on guard. The dinner had gone! He had been outwitted!

"The Speckledy Hen was very thin and scraggy, I'm sure," he told himself. "She wasn't worth eating. I am certain she was a tough fowl, and the chickens too."

He galloped away through the long woods, and over the river to his den in the far valley. Under his arm he carried the little book of Fables.

"I shall look at these pictures when I am hungry," he said. He settled himself in his rocking-chair and spelled out the story of "The Fox and the Grapes".

"She was very tough, that Speckledy Hen," said he.

"Three cheers for little Fuzzypeg," cried the Cock when Fuzzypeg finished telling them how he saved the Speckledy Hen.

"Hip, Hip, Hip, Hurrah!" they all cried and the Cock called, "Cockadoodle-doo-doo!" so loudly it rang across the wood to the ears of the Fox in his den.

"It all comes of being a scollard and going to school," said Old Hedgehog.

"Now I will make my cake," said Grey Rabbit. "We will have a feast for the Speckledy Hen and her family, and for brave little Fuzzypeg."